First American edition published in 2013 by Enchanted Lion Books
20 Jay Street, Studio M-18, Brooklyn, NY 11201
Copyright © 2013 by Enchanted Lion Books for this reprint edition.
Originally published in English in 1949 by J.B. Lippincott Company, Philadelphia and New York.
Copyright © by Isobel Harris for the text.
Copyright © by Pierre Farkas and Katherine Farkas-Kemmet for the illustrations of André François.
Rights for the illustrations negotiated with Éditions MeMo.
All rights reserved under International and Pan-American Copyright Conventions
ISBN 978-1-59270-135-3
Printed in March 2013 by South China Printing Company

# LITTLE BOY BROWN

*By Isobel Harris*

*Illustrated by André François*

DEDICATED TO
ANTHONY, PATRICIA AND DIANA

ENCHANTED LION BOOKS
NEW YORK

My mother is Mrs. Brown and my father is Mr. Brown—that's why I'm little boy Brown. I'm four and a half years old.

WE live in the City. It's easy the way we live, because we live in a hotel that has a tunnel all the way to the station and the Subway trains: And the Subway trains go right into the building where my father works, so he doesn't ever have to go out of doors at all.

4

My mother goes on a Subway train too, right into the very shop where she works. So she doesn't ever have to go out of doors either.

I AM the only one who ever goes out of doors into the fresh air. When my mother and my father go out they get a cold. I think maybe they should only go in the tunnels.

My friends are all the elevator men and the doormen and the waiters and, most of all, Hilda, the chambermaid. She is my favorite friend. Everyone takes turns taking me out. They like it. Mostly they have to take dogs out but we haven't a dog. We only have me.

Once when Hilda took me out it was the nicest time in all my life. This is what happened:

O<small>NE</small> morning at breakfast mother said: "How would you like to spend the whole day out in the country with Hilda?" I said it would be all right, because I like Hilda, and just then Hilda came in and she didn't have on her apron, but her hat and coat because it was her day off and she had come to the city just to get me. My mother and my father kissed me goodbye and they went to work. Then Hilda told me to hurry and get into my warmest winter clothes. She said it was cold. Our hotel is never cold.

HILDA was right! When we got in the elevator, John, the elevator man, said: "You'd better be careful of Jack Frost."

Eddy, the doorman, was standing inside because Jack Frost had bitten his nose. Jack Frost would have nipped Hilda and me too, if a Bus hadn't come along. Inside the Bus it was as warm as our hotel, only I think it was a little warmer.

We rode and we rode and we rode. We went as far as the Bus would go and when we got out what do you think happened?

A Policeman met us!

Hilda has a Policeman right in her family. It's her brother. He drove us in an automobile that wasn't a Taxi, right up to the little house where Hilda lives.

THE front door wasn't locked and we opened the door and walked right in. Hilda's mother kissed me before she even knew who I was!

HILDA'S house is wonderful! It has upstairs for bedrooms and downstairs for the kitchen and living-room. There is no elevator, only the stairs to walk up and down. I walked up and down eleven times.

In the living-room there is a fireplace that really burns and Hilda let me go with her to the woodpile by the back door and we carried in wood to burn.

THEN I took off my hat and coat and ran into the kitchen and watched Hilda's mother be a cook, and she made a cake and put chocolate frosting on it, and she made too much frosting and I had to eat it up for her. She said that if I hadn't been there it might have been wasted!

WHILE Hilda and her mother work they keep listening to their canary bird who sings to them. He doesn't have to stay in his cage. He flies all over the house and if he feels like it he sits on your head or on your hand. He is a very friendly bird.

Hilda has a dog, too. He doesn't go out on a leash, but all the time, any time, whenever he feels like it, and he goes out alone. He has long ears and a cold nose and the minute he saw me he put his head on my lap and we were friends.

At twelve o'clock Hilda's father came home from his Grocery shop to have his lunch. Hilda's family is smarter than we are. They can all speak two different languages, and they can close their eyes and think about two different countries. They've been on the Ocean, and they've climbed high mountains. They are very wonderful people. They haven't got quite enough of anything. It makes it exciting when a little more comes!

AFTER lunch while Hilda was clearing up the dishes, it began to snow. Big clean white snow. Even when it got on the ground it was white. The wind blew and the fires in the fireplace and the kitchen stove crackled brighter than ever. The snow splashed all over the window-panes and made jewels and lace.

Hilda's mother sat by the fire in the living-room and knit a stocking. I sat beside her and told her a story.

I told her that my mother and father were working hard so that some day they could take me across the Ocean where I could see all the things Hilda had seen and learn to do all the things that Hilda could do.

WHEN the house was all tidied up, Hilda's brother came home and he said: "Well now, why don't we all go out and make a Snowman?"

I hurried into my warm winter clothes again and we went out, and sure enough there was plenty of snow, and we all made a Snowman. We put a pipe in his mouth and a hat on his head and when he was finished we called him Mister Snow.

MISTER Snow hadn't been finished a minute when Hilda's mother opened the door and called: "Tea is ready!" We were certainly glad, because we knew there was the chocolate cake in the house. I had milk and bread and butter too. It was the first time I had ever had a Policeman with my tea. It made it better.

THEN it was time for me to go back to my hotel and I felt ... *Oh dear me!* ... That's how I felt.

Hilda thought I was tired, but I was only thinking ... *Oh dear me!* ... So I had to say goodbye.

HILDA's brother drove us to the Bus. It was empty and we were the only people who got in. Hilda's brother knew the driver and he told him about me being his friend, so we shook hands before we started.

PRETTY soon other people got into the Bus, so Hilda and I stopped acting friends with the driver and we started acting like passengers. It was fun because nobody guessed how well I knew the driver.

As we drove into the city we met trucks and men clearing away all the beautiful snow, and when we were right in the middle of the city there wasn't any snow left to be cleared away!

The Bus was so crowded that when it was time for us to get off, my friend the driver couldn't even *see* me to say goodbye.

At our hotel the doorman was so busy I couldn't tell about my day.

The elevator was full of brand new people, so John, the elevator man, had to give me his Excuse-me-I'm-busy wink.

HILDA had promised Mother she would undress me and put me to bed because Mother and Daddy were staying out late for dinner.

Pretty soon she thought that I was asleep and she tiptoed away. I was glad because I wanted to pretend I was still at Hilda's house.

*It was such a wonderful day!*

# The End

A NOTE ON THE TYPE

This book is set in Bulmer, a typeface designed by Ron Carpenter and issued by Monotype in 1930. It is named after William Bulmer, an English book printer of the late-eighteenth century, and is based on typefaces cut by William Martin in the 1790s.